Stubborn
Little
Pony

Titles in the Series

POP HOOPER'S
PERFECT PETS

Stubborn Little Pony

KYLE MEWBURN

ILLUSTRATED BY **HEATH MCKENZIE**

LITTLE HARE
www.littleharebooks.com

Little Hare Books
an imprint of
Hardie Grant Egmont
85 High Street
Prahran, Victoria 3181, Australia

www.littleharebooks.com

Text copyright © Kyle Mewburn 2010
Illustrations copyright © Heath McKenzie 2010

First published in 2010

National Library of Australia
Cataloguing-in-Publication entry

Mewburn, Kyle, 1963-

Stubborn little pony / Kyle Mewburn ;
illustrator, Heath McKenzie

978 1 921541 39 1 (pbk.)

For primary school age.

McKenzie, Heath.

NZ823.3

Cover design by Natalie Winter
Set in 13.5/24.5 pt Stone Informal by Clinton Ellicott
Printed by Griffin Press
Printed in Adelaide, Australia, June, 2010

5 4 3 2 1

This product conforms to CPSIA 2008

For Josh, the book-eating boy—KM

To Uncle Charlie's pony (whose name sadly escapes me), the only pony I ever got to ride and one that spookily fits the exact description of Popcorn! Perfect inspiration!—HMcK

One

Jake snatched up another box and flipped it upside down. Fishing rods, reels and tackle boxes tumbled out. One tackle box burst open, spilling lures, floats and brightly coloured flies everywhere. Jake didn't stop to pick them up. He dropped the empty box onto the pile of possessions littering his bedroom floor.

Then Jake grabbed a new box. 'My badminton racquet must be here somewhere,' he muttered.

Jake tipped over the box and shook it. A saddle fell out, followed by a tangle of bridles and other riding gear.

If Jake had labelled his boxes like his mum suggested, he would have found his racquet right away. But when his family moved to the city, Jake had just chucked all his belongings in together. He decided he wouldn't need any of it, because he would never go fishing or riding again. He didn't want the city kids thinking he was a country bumpkin.

When his dad got the new job training horses at a posh city riding school, Jake was excited. He imagined the city would be like the cities on TV, with lots of neon lights, mirrored skyscrapers and wailing police sirens. There would be massive video arcades and ice-cream shops selling a million flavours. Best of all, there would be lots of boys his age to play with. He'd soon have loads of new friends.

But the city wasn't like that at all. At least not in the riverside estate where Jake lived. The exciting city centre was across the river. On Jake's side there were just rows of tall apartment buildings. There were no arcades, no exciting shops and no ice-cream parlours. And Jake hadn't made a single friend.

But that might change ... if he could just find his stupid racquet!

Ever since Jake had moved to the city, he'd been waiting for a chance to play with Denny alone. Denny was the only boy Jake's age in the whole apartment block. He lived in the apartment directly below Jake's. Jake was sure they'd be friends—if only he could figure out what city boys like Denny liked to do.

When Jake overheard Denny telling his mum he was going up to the roof to play badminton, he couldn't believe his ears. He never imagined Denny liked playing badminton, too.

That was why he *had to* find his racquet. And fast!

Jake tipped over a long, skinny box. A telescope and a fishing net with an extendable pole slid out. But something stayed wedged inside. Jake scrunched the box, then gave it a shake.

His badminton racquet clattered onto the pile.

'Yes!' Jake shouted. He snatched up the racquet, then hurried out of his front door, down the corridor and up the apartment block's fire stairs.

As he ran, he swished his racquet through the air. His heart danced with excitement. Things were going to be so much better once he and Denny were friends!

Jake was bored silly with hanging around their seventh-floor apartment. In the country, he was always out riding or fishing. But his mum wouldn't let him explore the city alone.

Jake paused at the top of the fire stairs. Sometimes he sorely missed the farm.

A narrow path skirted the back wall of the roof, behind a row of shabby laundry rooms. On the other side, between the lift and several rows of washing lines, was a rectangle of concrete, covered in plastic grass. It was just big enough for a badminton court.

The swoosh of a badminton racquet drew Jake along the path like a magnet.

There's nothing to be nervous about, Jake told himself. But his hands were sweaty. He wasn't sure he was brave enough to play badminton up there. First hit, he'd probably send the shuttlecock sailing over the roof's edge.

'Great catch, Pete!' Denny's voice rang out across the roof.

Jake's heart sank. He should have known Denny wouldn't be playing alone.

SWOOSH! The racquet sliced the air again, sending a shuttlecock soaring above the laundry rooms. A moment later, there was a loud '*SQUAWK!*' and a rainbow-coloured parrot somersaulted into the air. It snatched the shuttlecock in its beak.

Blinking in surprise, Jake peeked around the corner.

'Good boy, Pete!' cheered Denny as the parrot landed on his shoulder. 'We're sure to win the Best Pet trophy at Pet Day!'

'*SQUAWK!*' the parrot said again.

Jake smiled. The next day at school was Pet Day. It would be such a fun day if Jake and Denny were friends. Jake could even help Denny train Pete.

But they weren't friends—yet.

Jake fumbled with his racquet. It was now or never.

He took a deep breath . . .

Just then, a thunderous roar set the building trembling beneath Jake's feet. A huge vehicle must have been rumbling past on the street below.

Denny ignored the noise. His racquet swept upwards again.

The rumbling got louder.

'What *is* making that sound?' Jake shouted.

Denny jumped at the sound
of Jake's voice, and mis-hit his
shuttlecock. It careened over the edge
of the roof. Denny turned and spotted
Jake. Then his face went bright red,
and he scuttled into the lift, with Pete
bobbing on his shoulder.

Jake was puzzled by Denny's
behaviour, and he didn't think to run
after him right away.

The building must rumble all the time, Jake thought. *That's why Denny didn't answer when I asked him about the noise. He probably thought I made him jump on purpose! No wonder he was angry.*

Jake chewed his lip. *If I try to explain,* he thought, *Denny will think I'm a lame country bumpkin who is scared of loud noises. But if I don't explain, we might never be friends.*

Suddenly a loud 'HOOT! HOOT!' echoed up from the street. Jake hurried over to the wall and looked downwards.

The longest, shiniest truck he'd ever seen was rumbling along the narrow street far below.

Written on the roof of each wagon in large, gold letters were the words: *Pop Hooper's Pet Express. Perfect Pets Guaranteed!*

That's what was making the noise! Jake thought. He forgot about explaining to Denny that he hadn't meant to startle him. He had a much better idea.

Imagine if Jake turned up to Pet Day with a parrot just like Denny's! Denny was sure to be impressed. Then they could play badminton together, while their parrots swooped and dived after their shuttlecocks. Finally, Jake would fit into his new life in the city.

But first he had to catch that truck!

Two

Jake flew down the fire stairs. At each landing he peered out the window to the street below. Luckily the truck had rumbled to a standstill.

It must be stuck at those traffic lights Dad's always complaining about, thought Jake. His father often complained that the lights on the corner took a long time to turn green.

As Jake reached the third-floor landing, the truck began to move again. Jake pelted down the final flights, three steps at a time. He had to catch that truck and get his parrot!

Jake burst through the ground-floor fire door and stumbled onto the street. The way ahead was crowded with fans returning home from a

football match nearby. The road was clogged with cars trailing streamers in team colours, and the pavement was full of people singing football songs.

The huge truck made the ground shake like an earthquake. But nobody noticed. That was strange.

Or was it? Maybe only country bumpkins like Jake got excited about such things. Perhaps everyone would laugh at Jake if they knew how excited he was about the pet truck.

Jake's racquet clattered to the ground as he pushed through the crowd, but he didn't stop to pick it up. He raced past boarded-up shops that were painted with graffiti.

Each time he reached a gang of older kids hanging out on the steps of an apartment building, Jake ducked his head. He didn't want to see anyone sniggering at him.

The truck threaded its way through the streets, with Jake in hot pursuit. Several times he thought he'd lost sight of the huge vehicle. Then, each time, he glimpsed it ahead, caught at another set of traffic lights.

But, once the truck reached the motorway on-ramp, there would be no more traffic lights. The truck might turn left and rumble out of town. Or it might head right onto the bridge that crossed the river, and get swallowed by the city centre.

Either way, Jake would never catch it.

In desperation, Jake cut across an empty car park. He dodged his way through a minefield of potholes and burnt-out cars. Then he squeezed through a slit in a wire fence.

He reached the bottom of the motorway on-ramp, puffing like a steam engine. His forehead glistened with sweat and his cheeks were streaked with soot. His eyes scanned every vehicle as the traffic whizzed past.

There was no sign of the truck.

But then a flicker of silver *under* the bridge caught Jake's gaze.

He hardly dared to breathe as he hurried towards the river.

Three

Two sooty bridge footings stood on
the edge of the river like the boots of
a giant fisherman. Overhead, the
traffic crossing the bridge sounded
like thunder. The smell of exhaust
fumes filled Jake's nose as he
approached the patch of ground that
ran along the riverside, underneath
the bridge.

Jake spotted the truck ahead, parked in a huge semicircle. There was no sign of the driver, but Jake was not alone. The shadows swarmed with pets from the truck. An army of white rats played hide-and-seek in piles of litter. A tortoise pushed an empty lemonade can along with its nose. Lemurs rolled old car tyres across the concrete. Dogs sniffed at oily posts. And peacocks flashed their tails at the graffiti-covered walls.

Every kind of pet imaginable was there . . . except a parrot.

Jake chewed his lip. Maybe he could get a different pet instead? Maybe a snake? Or a tarantula? Or . . .

A doubt crept into Jake's mind.

He might think snakes were cool, but Denny might think that only a country bumpkin would choose a snake for a pet. Jake couldn't risk that. If he couldn't have a parrot, it was safer to have no pet at all.

Jake felt his hopes deflating.

Suddenly a snow-white cockatoo swooped down and landed on his shoulder.

'Ride 'em, cowboy!' it squawked.

Jake laughed. A talking cockatoo was a bit like a parrot! It would be the perfect pet to take to Pet Day. And it would give Jake the perfect excuse to hang out with Denny, too.

Now all he had to do was find the cockatoo's owner. 'Hello?' he called.

A strange whistling sound drew
Jake's eyes upwards. He spotted a
man with a shiny silver suit and a
curly silver moustache. The man was
swinging from a trapeze slung from
the girders of the bridge overhead.
He whizzed by close enough to ruffle
Jake's hair.

Jake stared. The trapeze soared past. Suddenly, the man let go of the trapeze bar and somersaulted into thin air.

Jake gasped. He hardly dared watch.

The man tumbled once . . . twice . . . then plummeted earthwards. He landed beside Jake with a low bow.

'Pop Hooper at your service,' said the man, smiling. 'What can I do for a young city slicker like you?'

Jake felt himself getting tongue-tied. Nobody had ever mistaken him for a city kid before. Finally he blurted: 'Please can I have this cockatoo for a pet?'

'Marshmallow's old enough to make his own decisions. Why don't you ask him?' said Mister Hooper.

Jake licked his lips nervously. 'Do you want to come home with me, Marshmallow?' he asked the bird.

'No place like home!' squawked Marshmallow. He fluttered onto Mister Hooper's shoulder.

'Marshmallow doesn't have to be my pet, I suppose,' said Jake, trying to hide his disappointment. 'Any parrot would be fine, as long as it can talk or do tricks. Denny's parrot, Pete, catches shuttlecocks in midair.'

'Parrots won't take orders from just anyone,' said Mister Hooper kindly. 'They have to get to know you first.'

'But it's an emergency!' Jake insisted. 'If I don't have a cool parrot to take to Pet Day tomorrow, I won't get a chance to impress Denny. And then we'll *never* be friends, and I'll be stuck by myself in this city forever.'

Mister Hooper scratched his chin. 'That's not a very good reason to want a parrot, young man,' he said. 'Or any pet, for that matter. A pet is a wonderful friend. And it's never a good idea to use one friend to impress another.'

'I *knew* the sign on your truck was too good to be true,' Jake muttered, scuffing up dust with his shoe.

'Too true to be good!' said Marshmallow.

Jake was surprised when the old man chuckled.

'Don't be silly,' said Mister Hooper. 'We'll have your perfect pet sorted in no time. It's guaranteed, remember? Now, wait here.'

Jake was confused, but he was excited, too. Mister Hooper *did* mean he would find Jake a pet parrot ... didn't he?

Slowly, Jake became aware of a clip-clopping sound behind him. The sound got closer. Then something snuffled beside his ear. Jake turned around ...

... and stumbled back as a pony snorted warm, moist air right into his face.

'Hello, pony!' smiled Jake, stroking
the pony's head.

The pony shook its mane and
whinnied. It was the scruffiest pony
Jake had ever seen. It was covered
with brown and white splotches.
It had a white tail and a long, white
mane which covered its eyes.

The pony nuzzled Jake's chest. Jake grabbed its halter.

Mister Hooper appeared from behind the trucks. 'That pony's name is Popcorn,' he said. 'He likes you! I knew he would!'

Jake's free hand ruffled Popcorn's mane, but his eyes eagerly scanned the parking place. There was no sign of his parrot.

'Don't look so glum, Jake,' said Mister Hooper. 'Finding a perfect pet sometimes takes a little time. And finding a tricksy parrot can be especially tricky.'

'Trick or treat!' squawked Marshmallow.

'Pet Day is tomorrow!' Jake cried.

Mister Hooper smiled. 'Don't worry, Jake. You'll have your perfect pet in plenty of time. In the meantime, Popcorn needs someone to look after him for the night. Someone who knows a thing or two about ponies. So I was wondering ...?'

Jake realised that Mister Hooper was asking if Jake would take Popcorn home with him. He shook his head. It was true that Jake had been good with ponies when he lived on the farm. But the last thing he needed now was for Denny to see him with a pony, like some silly country bumpkin!

'You'd be doing me a favour,' said Mister Hooper.

'But where would I keep him?' Jake groaned. He glanced at Popcorn.

The pony's mane was tangled and his coat was dusty. He needed a good wash and a brush. Jake could never turn up at his dad's riding school with such a scruffy pony. The other horses were well-groomed thoroughbreds. Jake would be a laughing-stock!

Popcorn snorted, then bent to nuzzle Jake's shoelaces.

'You'll think of something, Jake,' said Mister Hooper. 'It's just for one night. And you'll have your perfect pet before you know it.'

Jake squirmed. Mister Hooper was crazy to think that the city was any place for a pony!

But finally, Jake nodded. He'd do anything for a parrot like Denny's.

'It's a deal then, Jake!' Mister Hooper hooted. 'You take Popcorn for the night, and I'll see you back here tomorrow morning, with your perfect pet!'

Jake slowly led Popcorn out from underneath the bridge. Something was bothering him. Try as he might, he couldn't remember telling Mister Hooper his name.

Four

Jake's face was hot as he led Popcorn
back through the housing estate.
What a stupid country boy he
must look, walking a pony along
the city streets! It took forever for the
lights to change at each pedestrian
crossing. The football fans who
were waiting to cross kept asking
Jake if they could stroke Popcorn.

They thought Popcorn was his!

Popcorn shook his mane and nickered contentedly.

Eventually Jake and the pony turned into Jake's street. Jake glimpsed a red-haired figure ahead. It looked like it might be Denny. Jake's throat tightened. He couldn't let Denny catch him with Popcorn. Jake might as well wear a cowboy hat and a T-shirt saying: *One Hundred Percent Country Bumpkin.*

Jake turned around. 'Come on, Popcorn. I'm taking you back to Mister Hooper,' he said. He'd rather Denny was still cross with him about the lost shuttlecock than laughing at him for having a pony in the city.

Popcorn refused to budge.

Jake wrapped his arms around Popcorn's neck and tried to wrestle the pony into facing the right way. Popcorn tossed his head and sent Jake tumbling onto the pavement.

Jake huffed in frustration.

Popcorn bent down and shoved Jake with his muzzle.

'Leave me alone,' Jake grumbled, squirming along the pavement.

Popcorn gave him another shove.

Jake scrambled to his feet. He glanced down the street, half-expecting to see Denny standing there, laughing at him. But the kid with the red hair had gone. Jake turned and gave Popcorn an icy stare.

Popcorn stared back calmly, blinking his long eyelashes.

'Leave. Me. *Alone,*' Jake ordered the pony. He turned away and marched towards home. When Jake heard Popcorn's hooves clip-clopping behind him, he swung around and waved his arms wildly. 'Go away! Shoo! Scram!'

Popcorn stepped closer and nickered again.

Jake sighed in defeat. He was stuck with the pony for the night. And he could only think of one place to hide Popcorn: on the roof of Jake's apartment building. But he'd be taking a huge risk. He'd have to sneak Popcorn past Mister Althrop, the apartment block's caretaker. And he'd have to hope Denny didn't play badminton with Pete the parrot up on the roof again.

It was going to be a long night.

*

Jake hid Popcorn behind a rubbish skip opposite his apartment building. When the last of the football-crowd stragglers had passed, he pulled on Popcorn's halter. The two of them trotted across the street and up the front steps. Popcorn's tiny hooves rang out on the marble floor as they clattered across the foyer.

Jake yanked open the door to the fire stairs. But Popcorn refused to walk through it.

'*Move*, or we'll get caught!' hissed Jake, slapping Popcorn's rump.

Popcorn whinnied loudly.

Jake squeezed Popcorn's muzzle shut. 'All right. We'll use the lift,' he said.

Jake held his breath as he heard the lift approaching. Finally the doors slid open . . .

The lift was empty.

'Phew!' Jake said. He hurried Popcorn inside and waited for the doors to close. As the lift glided upwards, Jake's eyes were glued to the glowing numbers.

First floor . . . Second floor . . . Third floor . . . Fourth floor . . . Fifth floor . . .

If anyone saw Jake with Popcorn, they'd tell Jake's parents, and Jake's parents would make Jake take Popcorn back to Mister Hooper. Then Jake wouldn't get his parrot. And if he missed his chance to impress Denny at Pet Day, he'd probably end up staying friendless the whole year. Maybe forever!

Sixth floor . . . Seventh floor . . .

Eighth floor ... Ninth floor ... Tenth floor ...

The lift doors opened. Jake scanned the roof. Rows of washing swayed gently in the breeze. Nobody lurked in the laundry rooms. The coast was clear.

Jake led Popcorn across the plastic grass to the wooden picnic bench which was squeezed against the far wall of the roof. He tethered the pony to the bench with some washing line. Popcorn lifted his head and whinnied loudly.

'Stay here and be quiet,' Jake said, wagging a finger at Popcorn. 'I have to go for dinner before Mum gets suspicious. I'll bring you some food and water later. But if you cause any trouble, I'll take you back to Mister Hooper faster than you can say neigh. I won't risk Denny seeing me with a dumb, scruffy pony like *you*.'

He left Popcorn snorting along the plastic grass.

Five

Jake's stomach gurgled nervously all through dinner. His mind raced with thoughts. What if someone from his apartment block went up to the roof to collect their laundry? Or what if Mister Althrop had to inspect something up there? Or, worst of all, what if Denny decided to play badminton with Pete again?

Jake wolfed down his dinner, then leapt to his feet.

'I'm going up to the roof for some fresh air,' he said.

'Don't be long,' said his mum.

Jake sneaked some apples into his pockets, then hurried to the lift.

*

As soon as the lift doors opened, Jake groaned. Popcorn was gone! The tether was swinging from the picnic bench. Somehow, the pony had managed to undo Jake's knot.

'Popcorn!' Jake hissed, creeping forwards.

A soft nicker drew him towards the shadows beside the lift shaft.

'I know you're there,' Jake said.

He fished an apple from his pocket and crept closer. 'I've got a nice, crunchy apple for you.'

Popcorn stepped forwards and swung his muzzle, knocking the apple from Jake's grasp.

'What did you do that for?' Jake asked, scurrying to retrieve it.

Popcorn followed him. As soon as Jake was bending down, Popcorn gave him a hearty shove, and sent Jake sprawling headfirst into a sheet hanging from a clothes line. By the time Jake untangled himself, Popcorn was standing just out of reach, munching on the apple. There was a mischievous twinkle in the pony's eyes.

Jake scrambled to his feet. 'Come here this instant, or I'll . . . I'll . . .' His mind whirred desperately. But he kept drawing a blank. Really, there was nothing he *could* do. He was stuck with Popcorn.

Popcorn whinnied. Jake knew the pony was laughing at him. That was the final straw. Jake would not let a

stupid pony get the better of *him*! He lunged. Popcorn danced away from his grasp.

Jake stumbled into the metal pole that held up the washing line. It clattered to the ground, bringing rows of washing swooping down around Jake. They tangled round his legs. He toppled to the floor like a lassoed calf.

Popcorn trotted merrily in circles, just out of Jake's reach. His hooves rang out like gunshots. Someone was bound to hear. Jake felt like fleeing. But he didn't have the strength to move. He lay in a heap, waiting to be discovered, wishing he'd never set eyes on the annoying pony.

He heard hooves clip-clopping closer. Then warm breath snorted through his shirt as Popcorn nuzzled his pockets. Jake sighed. He *had* to get his parrot. And that meant putting up with this stupid pony till morning whether he liked it or not.

Jake untangled himself from the washing line and fished an apple from his pocket. Popcorn sniffed

Jake's hand, then crunched up the apple. Juice and slobber dribbled through Jake's fingers.

Once Popcorn had eaten all the apples, Jake led him back to the plastic lawn and tethered him to the bench again. This time, he used a complicated knot. Then Jake filled a bucket with water from a laundry room and brought it to the pony. While Popcorn slurped thirstily, Jake stared at the city lights flickering on the other side of the river.

It's not long till morning, he thought. *And then all my problems will be over.*

He hardly noticed that his hand was stroking Popcorn's mane.

Six

Jake tossed and turned all night.
He was too excited to sleep. Pet Day
would be so much fun once he had
a parrot like Denny's. And Jake and
Denny would be great friends once
Denny realised Jake wasn't a country
bumpkin after all.

As dawn broke, Jake jumped out of
bed and dressed quickly. When he

saw his old riding gear on the floor,
he scooped it up. It would be
embarrassing riding Popcorn through
the estate, but it would be quicker
than leading him. And the sooner he
returned Popcorn to Pop Hooper and
got his parrot, the better!

He was halfway to the front
door when his parents' bedroom door
opened.

'Where are you going, Jake?' asked
his mum. 'And why are you carrying
your saddle?'

'I ... I ... I ...' Jake stuttered.

Then the bathroom door
opened. 'What's going on here?'
said Jake's dad.

Seeing his dad gave Jake an idea.

'Dad said if I ever wanted to go riding, I could visit him at work on the way home from school,' he told his mum. 'Didn't you, Dad?' he added.

'Sure did,' his dad replied. 'We don't want you getting rusty. You're a good rider.'

Jake's mum eyed Jake suspiciously. 'I thought you said you never wanted to ride again, because riding was for country bumpkins?'

Jake blushed. 'I changed my mind,' he said.

His mum was about to quiz him further, when his dad's voice floated out from the bathroom. 'We're out of toothpaste!'

'There's some in the cabinet!' Jake's mum said. She swept down the hall with her dressing-gown flapping behind her. 'I'll get it!'

Jake put the last few apples from the fruit bowl into his schoolbag. Then he made his getaway.

*

When the lift doors opened onto the roof, Jake felt like pulling his hair out. Popcorn had got loose again, even though Jake had tied everything extra tight.

As Jake plonked his riding gear on the picnic bench, he glimpsed the end of Popcorn's tether trailing behind the laundry rooms. Jake gritted his teeth. He'd had enough of the stupid pony already and the day had hardly begun!

Jake stormed across the roof. As he bent to pick up the tether, Popcorn's tail lashed out, catching Jake in the mouth. While Jake spluttered, Popcorn whinnied and wheeled away from him.

'No, you don't!' Jake cried. He threw himself forwards and grabbed the tether just in time. 'Got you!'

Popcorn snorted in protest all the way to the picnic bench. But Jake was in no mood to listen. He hooked the tether around the leg of the bench and held out an apple to Popcorn. 'This should keep you quiet,' he said.

While Popcorn munched the apple, Jake threw the saddle cloth over the pony's back. Popcorn was still chomping away as Jake put the saddle on top of the saddle cloth. He was relieved when the girth band that held the saddle in place was fastened securely. For some reason, he hadn't expected the saddle to fit.

Jake slid the bridle over Popcorn's muzzle. But he didn't remove the halter until the bridle was firmly buckled. As Jake slid the halter free, he made sure he had a firm hold of the reins. He expected Popcorn to make a dash for it. But the pony bent to snuffle the plastic grass.

'C'mon, Popcorn,' said Jake, tugging the reins. 'Let's get you back to Mister Hooper so I can pick up my parrot before school starts.'

Popcorn dug his hooves into the plastic lawn.

'I haven't got time for this,' Jake grumbled.

Popcorn bent down and nuzzled the empty water bucket.

Jake sighed. 'All right, I'll get you some water. But then we're leaving.'

Before he went to fetch the water, Jake looped the reins securely around the bench leg, so Popcorn couldn't run off. He wasn't taking *any* chances!

Jake returned with an overflowing bucket. While Popcorn drank, Jake walked across to the lift and pressed the call button. Then he walked back to Popcorn, unhitched the reins and waited impatiently for the pony to finish.

BING! The lift arrived. The doors slowly opened.

'Hurry up,' Jake muttered, tugging on Popcorn's reins.

Popcorn nickered, then sent the
bucket tumbling with a sweep of his
head. Water splashed everywhere!
Jake leapt aside, trying to keep his
shoes from being soaked. He landed
awkwardly on the wet plastic grass.
His feet slipped out from beneath
him. His hands flew backwards to
cushion his fall . . .

. . . and he let go of the reins.

Popcorn darted towards the lift.

'Come back!' shouted Jake. He tried to scramble to his feet. But he kept slipping. As he sprawled onto his stomach, he caught one last glimpse of Popcorn before the lift doors shut.

The lift started descending.

*

Shouts and cries erupted from the foyer as Jake plunged down the fire stairs.

He burst into the foyer. Everything was in uproar. Pot plants were tipped over. Armchairs were scattered willy-nilly. The ground-floor tenants were spilling out of their apartments.

Mister Althrop stood by the lift.

He was scowling at a steaming pile of manure. Popcorn pranced away down the front steps, swinging his mane.

When Mister Althrop saw Jake, his face turned red.

Jake rushed out through the door.

Mister Althrop wasn't far behind. 'I want a word with you!' he growled.

Jake leapt onto Popcorn's back and kicked him into a canter. 'Let's get out of here!' he said to the pony.

The pavement was crowded with Monday-morning commuters heading towards the train station, and with children walking to school. A knot of men in blue overalls leapt aside as Popcorn clattered past.

'Hold your horses!' one of them yelled at Jake's back. His friends hooted with laughter.

'Yee-ha!' sniggered a skateboarder with a nose-ring.

Jake stared straight ahead. If anyone from his school saw him riding a pony along the street, he'd be a laughing-stock. Then Denny would never be friends with him, even once Jake had his own parrot!

Seven

The bridge arches loomed into view.
Jake sighed with relief. The worst was
over! He'd ditch this pain of a pony,
collect his parrot, and still get to
school before Pet Day started. He
couldn't wait to see Denny's face.

As they galloped past the gates of
the riverside park, Jake kept Popcorn's
head facing straight ahead and

kicked him on, in case Popcorn made a dash for the gates. The park's lush, green grass looked very inviting. But Popcorn headed obediently towards the bridge. He seemed keen to get back to Mister Hooper, too.

The truck was still parked in a semicircle on the oil-stained dirt. But the wagons were all shut. There were no pets loose. And there was no sign of Mister Hooper.

I hope he didn't forget about my parrot, thought Jake as he dismounted.

Suddenly, a loud *'SQUAWK!'* echoed off the river. Jake tied Popcorn's reins to the bars of a wagon, and hurried towards the sound.

Jake rounded the corner of a wagon. Mister Hooper was standing in front of him, holding a huge, rainbow-coloured parrot. Jake smiled. The parrot looked exactly like Pete. He was perfect!

'Can I hold him?' Jake burst out.

Mister Hooper laughed. 'Of course you can. Peanut's yours . . . if you want him.'

Marshmallow flew into view and settled on Mister Hooper's shoulder. 'Peanuts! Popcorn!' he squawked.

'Hello, Peanut,' said Jake, as the parrot clambered onto his arm.

'So when are you planning on returning Popcorn?' Mister Hooper asked.

Frowning, Jake glanced up. Popcorn was gone!

Then, suddenly, Jake glimpsed the runaway pony disappearing into the park.

'I'm sorry,' said Mister Hooper, taking Peanut back from Jake's wrist, 'but I can't let you have Peanut until you bring back Popcorn.'

*

Jake ran through the park, getting more frustrated with every step. Up ahead, Popcorn introduced himself to every jogger and rollerblader. Each time Popcorn halted, Jake doubled his pace. If he yelled, someone could easily grab Popcorn's reins. But the last thing Jake wanted was to draw attention to himself.

'Stupid pony,' Jake muttered. 'I was *so* close to getting my parrot.' He was about to give up, when Popcorn came to a sudden stop . . .

. . . right outside the riding school where Jake's dad worked!

Jake stood rooted to the spot with fear. He was stranded out in the open. There was nowhere to hide.

Inside the riding school, several children in spotless dressage costumes were lined up beside their horses on the edge of a sawdust arena. The horses' manes and tails were braided, and their riding gear gleamed. In the centre of the arena, a proud palomino pranced patterns in the sawdust. Jake's dad was sitting tall in the saddle, hardly moving a muscle.

Jake knew how much skill you needed to steer a horse like that. Before they moved to the city, Jake had imagined that he would grow up to be a horse trainer, too. Now he wasn't sure what he wanted to be. All he knew was that it wouldn't have anything to do with horses or ponies.

'Popcorn!' he hissed. 'Come here!'

When Popcorn reared up and whinnied loudly, Jake sprang into action. He had nothing to lose.

'*Yah!*' yelled Jake. Then he charged ahead, waving his arms wildly.

Popcorn got the message. He galloped off along the fence.

Jake sprinted behind, hoping desperately his dad hadn't seen him.

Eight

As Jake ran, he glimpsed a clump of
concrete buildings rising above the
trees ahead. His stomach churned
with dread. Popcorn was heading
straight for Jake's school. It was Jake's
worst nightmare!

Popcorn didn't quite make it into
the school grounds. A few metres
from the school's side gate, his reins

got hooked on a lawn sprinkler. He was nickering grumpily when Jake caught up.

Jake hurriedly grabbed Popcorn's reins. Maybe there was still time to get back to Mister Hooper and swap the pony for the parrot ...

The school bell started to ring.

Jake groaned. It was too late to take Popcorn back. And he couldn't

leave him tethered in the park, either. Anyone might take him. There was only one option. He had to find somewhere in the school grounds to hide Popcorn. Fast!

I can swap Popcorn for Peanut at lunchtime, Jake thought. *Pet Day won't be a total disaster if I have my parrot by the afternoon.*

Butterflies twittered in Jake's stomach as he led Popcorn through the gate. He navigated a zigzag path through a maze of tall buildings. The sounds of excited children and pets gathering outside the assembly hall echoed around the school. At every corner Jake held his breath, waiting to be discovered with the pony.

Finally he reached the school nature garden. It was a drab, dusty square filled with straggly plants, enclosed by a tall fence. Popcorn should stay safely hidden there ... at least until lunchtime.

The final bell sounded as Jake latched the gate. He hurriedly retraced his steps and joined the end of the line snaking into the assembly hall.

Inside the hall, teachers rushed around madly, untangling leads and settling quarrels between pet owners. Children were busily calming their own pets or inspecting their friends' pets. Dogs sniffed each other. Cats arched their backs and hissed.

Hamsters spun their wheels into a blur. Goldfish stared out of bowls. Tim Gunn's white rat poked a quivering nose out of his top pocket. Melissa Bond's turtle sat like a rock on the front of the stage.

Denny was sitting in the third row, with a badminton racquet in his lap and Pete perched on his shoulder. Jake sighed. If he had got Peanut like he'd planned, he could be sitting beside Denny right now.

Instead, he found a seat a couple of rows behind Denny.

Just a few more hours, he thought, *and then I'll have a parrot, too.*

It would be such a relief to finally get rid of that stupid pony.

Then Jake heard a sound.

Clip-clop . . . Clip-clop . . . Clip-clop . . .

Jake hoped he was dreaming. But there was no mistaking that noise. It got louder. And louder.

A cry of delight rang through the hall as Popcorn trotted through the doors. Children leapt to their feet and craned their necks, trying to get a better view of the pony intruder.

Jake glanced behind him. The emergency exit was three rows behind. His feet itched and he longed to dash out the door. But the aisles were blocked with classmates. He'd never make it in time.

'That pony is so cool!' Melody Asquith squealed.

'Who does it belong to?' Dylan Benson shouted.

'Everyone quieten down,' yelled Mrs Harmon.

'Back to your seats,' urged Mister Smither.

Nobody listened. They all crowded around Popcorn, muttering with excitement.

Popcorn plodded through the cluster of children and clopped up the middle aisle. Jake shrank deeper into his seat. Popcorn was heading straight towards him!

Every head turned to follow Popcorn's progress. Jake stared straight ahead. His face was hot with shame. It seemed to take forever for Popcorn to reach him.

Popcorn nickered loudly, then bent forward to nuzzle Jake's chest.

The hall erupted with laughter. Jake felt like crying.

Suddenly a shout exploded from near the stage. 'Pete! Come back!'

Everyone turned around. Gasps fizzed through the aisles as Denny's parrot fluttered to the front of the hall and disappeared through an open window.

'All the noise frightened him,' said Denny.

Children surged towards the window like a tidal wave. Mrs Harmon called for everyone to return to their seats. But nobody heard her.

Denny pushed and shoved at the children in his way, desperately trying to reach the door. But there was no way through the crowd.

Jake leapt to his feet. It was all Popcorn's fault that Pete was scared. 'You stupid pony!' he yelled, his face centimetres from Popcorn's. 'Pete could be lost forever!'

Popcorn nickered and pawed the ground. Suddenly, Jake had an idea. There was no time to waste!

Nine

Jake vaulted onto Popcorn's back.
He snatched up the reins and wheeled
Popcorn towards the emergency exit.
As they burst through the door, Jake
glimpsed Pete fluttering towards the
trees at the far end of the sports field.

The crowd of children poured
through the main doors and onto the
playground.

Denny led the way. 'Pete! Come back!' he yelled.

Jake's classmates stared at him as he charged past on Popcorn. They'd all know Jake was a country bumpkin now. But he didn't care. He had to save Pete.

'Go, boy!' Jake urged Popcorn.

They raced along the edge of the sports field, scanning the trees. Jake hoped Pete hadn't flown out of the school grounds.

Suddenly Popcorn dug in his hooves and wheeled around to face the way he had come.

'Where are you going, you stupid pony?' demanded Jake. He was about to tug Popcorn's reins when he

noticed a flicker of colour out of
the corner of his eye. There was Pete!
He was perched on a lower branch of
an oak tree.

Popcorn slowed to a walk and
quietly approached the tree. Jake
stood up on the saddle and held out
a hand. 'It's all right, Pete,' he said
soothingly to the parrot. 'I won't
hurt you.'

The parrot considered Jake's hand,
then spread his wings. Jake feared
Pete would fly off again and be lost
for good. Instead, he fluttered across
to Jake's outstretched wrist.

'Let's go, Popcorn,' said Jake,
sitting back into the saddle and
gently kicking the pony into a walk.

As they headed back to the hall,
Jake dared not move a muscle in case
Pete got scared. But Popcorn knew
exactly where to go.

*

Jake and Popcorn were swamped as
soon as they came to a halt. Denny
rushed forward to retrieve Pete.

'I think we all know who deserves

the Best Pet trophy this year!' cheered Mrs Harmon.

Jake glanced guiltily at Denny. Denny was sure to be disappointed he didn't win the trophy, and horrified that a country bumpkin like Jake had won it instead. Not only was it Popcorn's fault that Pete had been scared in the first place, the pony wasn't even Jake's pet!

He was surprised to see Denny cheering the loudest of all.

'Thanks for rescuing Pete,' said Denny.

'It was Popcorn's fault that he got scared in the first place,' said Jake.

'Nah,' said Denny. 'He was scared as soon as we all came into the hall.

He's not used to other pets or kids.
I should have trained him better.'

Jake was amazed. Denny hadn't blamed Jake for Pete flying away, *and* he was pleased that Jake had rescued Pete!

'That was some awesome riding!' whistled Denny, stroking Popcorn's mane. 'I wish I knew how to ride.'

Jake stared at Denny. He'd been so busy trying to impress Denny, he'd never imagined Denny might be interested in things Jake was actually good at. Such as riding.

'I can teach you ... if you like,' Jake stammered.

'Brilliant!' said Denny. 'You must miss living in the country.'

Jake laughed. 'Yeah, I do sometimes. But living in the city's pretty cool, too.' He licked his lips. 'Hey, do you want to play badminton later?'

Jake was surprised when Denny blushed. 'I'll probably smash it over the edge of the roof on my first hit. You saw how terrible I was yesterday.'

Jake smiled. Everything was OK! Denny hadn't even been angry with Jake about the lost shuttlecock. 'Maybe we could go to the park to play,' he said.

'That'd be cool,' said Denny. 'My mum doesn't let me go *anywhere* by myself.'

Jake began to wonder how the worst day ever had magically turned into the best day ever.

Suddenly a familiar voice boomed from the back of the crowd. 'That was some fancy riding, Jake!'

Jake saw his dad striding towards him, and his face fell. Mr Althrop must have told Dad about the manure in the foyer!

Jake's dad gave Jake a long, serious look . . . then burst out laughing. 'When I saw you chasing that pony past the riding school this morning, I thought I'd better come and see what you were up to,' he chuckled. 'I'm glad I did. I told your mum you weren't serious about giving up

riding. It's in the blood, hey, Jake? So
where'd you find this feisty little guy?'

'I'm looking after him for
someone,' said Jake. 'I was supposed
to give him back this morning,
but ...'

He swallowed hard as he realised
that returning Popcorn was the last
thing he wanted to do now.

He didn't want a parrot. Parrots were for city kids, not country bumpkins like Jake. 'Can we keep Popcorn?' he asked his dad.

Jake's dad smiled. 'If his owner agrees, I'll squeeze him in at the stables. He'll stop those horses getting big heads. I'll take him there now.'

'Thanks, Dad!' said Jake, wrapping his arms around Popcorn's neck.

All this time, Jake had thought Popcorn was a troublemaker. But, really, the pony was just being himself. Jake knew how hard that was! Popcorn might be scruffy and stubborn, but he was perfect for Jake.

Jake hoped Mister Hooper would let Popcorn stay with him.

Ten

After school, Jake and Denny hurried to the riding school. Jake couldn't wait to show Popcorn the Best Pet trophy they'd won together. When he saw his dad grooming Popcorn inside, he froze in amazement. Popcorn didn't look scruffy any more. He looked proud and dashing.

I'm so stupid, Jake thought sadly.

I should have realised ages ago that Popcorn was my perfect pet. Mister Hooper will never let him stay with me after all the trouble I've caused.

Suddenly, a loud '*HOOT! HOOT!*' echoed down the street.

When Mister Hooper's truck pulled up opposite the riding school, Jake's stomach gurgled with fear. Denny didn't seem to notice. He stood watching Popcorn with a rapt smile.

'Hi, Jake!' Mister Hooper called, as Jake hurried across the street. 'I thought I might find you here. I was wondering if you would do me a huge favour and let Popcorn stay here in the city with you.'

Jake's mouth fell open.

'I know you wanted a parrot,' Mister Hooper continued. 'But, well, I'm afraid poor old Peanut doesn't care for city life. He's more of a country bird. And Popcorn would be happy here with you. He loves the city. So, what do you say?'

Jake could only nod.

'Terrific!' hooted Mister Hooper.

'So, did you manage to impress your friend this morning?'

Jake blushed. 'I think so.'

'The best way to impress people is to be yourself,' said Mister Hooper with a wink. 'Right, Marshmallow?'

'Cock-a-doodle-doo!' crowed Marshmallow.

Jake watched Mister Hooper's truck rumble away. Then he raced back across the street. 'C'mon, Denny, let's go and feed Popcorn,' he yelled as he whizzed past. 'Last one there's a country bumpkin!'

'You've got no chance!' snorted Denny, close in pursuit.

And Jake didn't really care if he was last or not.